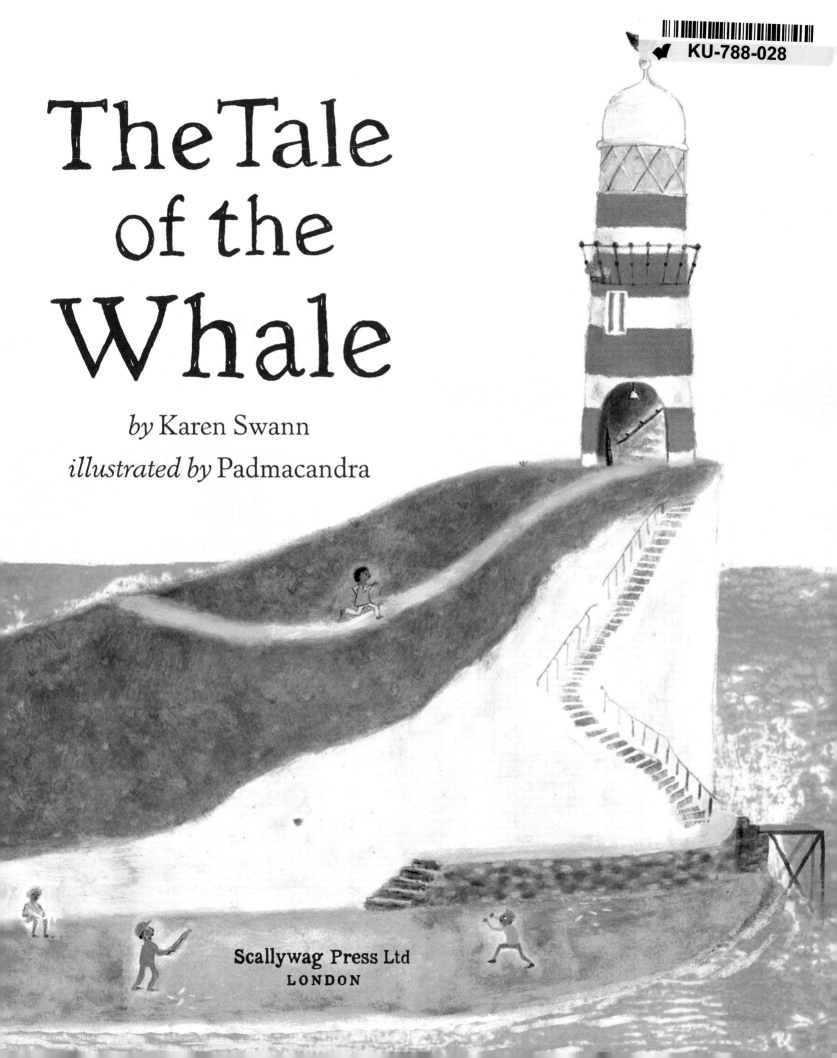

The Tale of the Whale

by Karen Swann

illustrated by Padmacandra

Scallywag Press Ltd

LONDON

Where land becomes sky
and the sky becomes sea,
I first saw the whale . . .

... and the whale first saw me.

And high on the breeze came his sweet-sounding song –

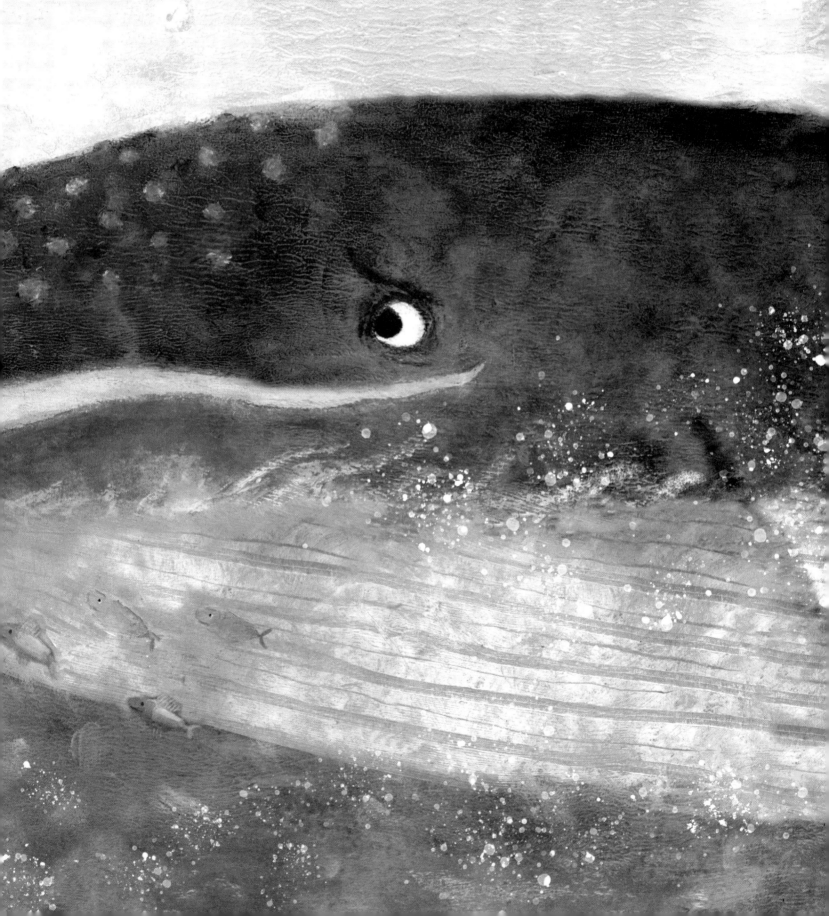

'I've so much to show you, if you'll come along.'

I scrambled aboard in the silvery light
And watched cliff-top houses drift far out of sight.
We floated away on the rocking-horse sea . . .

I smiled at the whale
and the whale smiled at me.

We sailed the blue ocean
with turtles and rays,
And tail-splashed the seagulls
in deep water bays.

We danced with the dolphins that waltzed through the sea . . .

I laughed with the whale

and the whale laughed with me.

I took a deep breath and we dived through the blue,
And there, on the bottom, a ship with no crew!

We ducked under arches, no treasure to see . . .

I shrugged at the whale and the whale shrugged at me.

We swam over mountains,
through valleys of sand –

An ocean in motion,
a bright busy land –

With carpets of colours that
breathed with the sea . . .

I watched with the whale
and the whale watched with me.

We crashed through the surface.
We splashed oh, so high –
A splutter, a rumble then 'whoosh' to the sky!

'I'm flying!' I cried
to the cold ice-capped sea . . .

I waved to the whale
and the whale waved to me.

The whale's tummy rumbled; his mouth opened wide
And half of an ocean was swallowed inside . . .

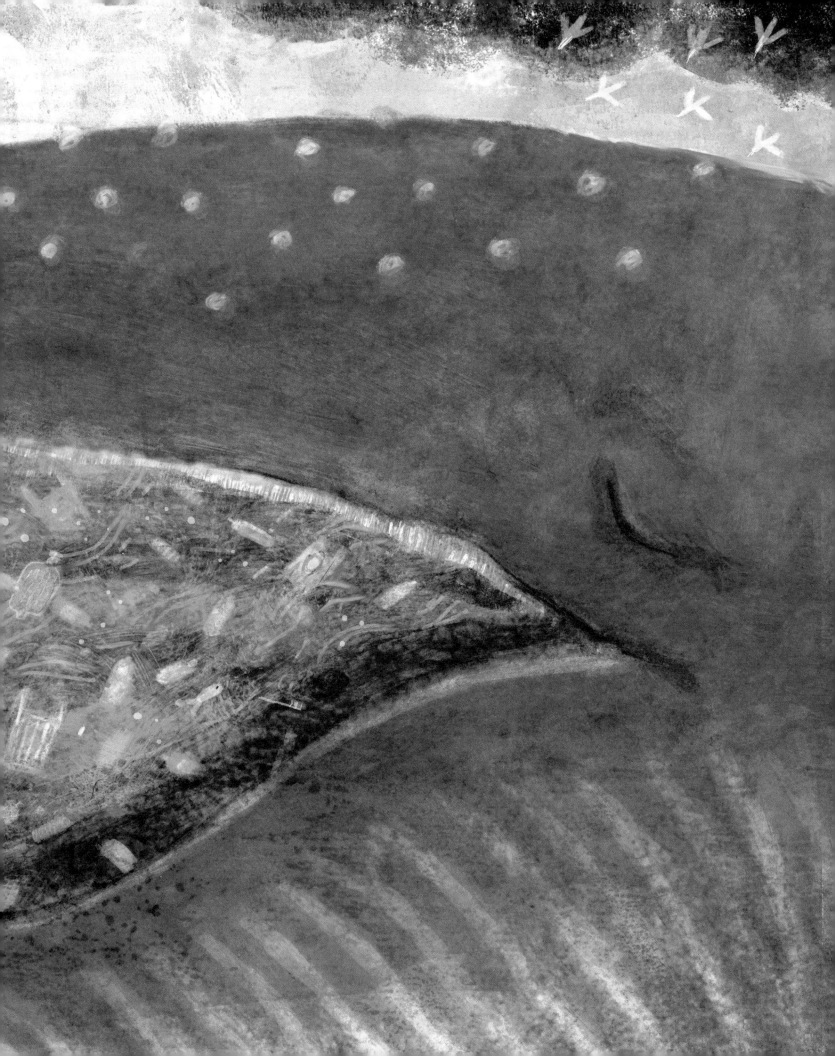

I stared at the whale
as he stared back at me –
I understood now what
he'd brought me to see:

An old water bottle, a toothbrush, a straw,
A crisp packet, fishing nets, ten bags or more;
Some food wrap and cartons, a large coffee cup –
The soup of the ocean, he'd swallowed it up;

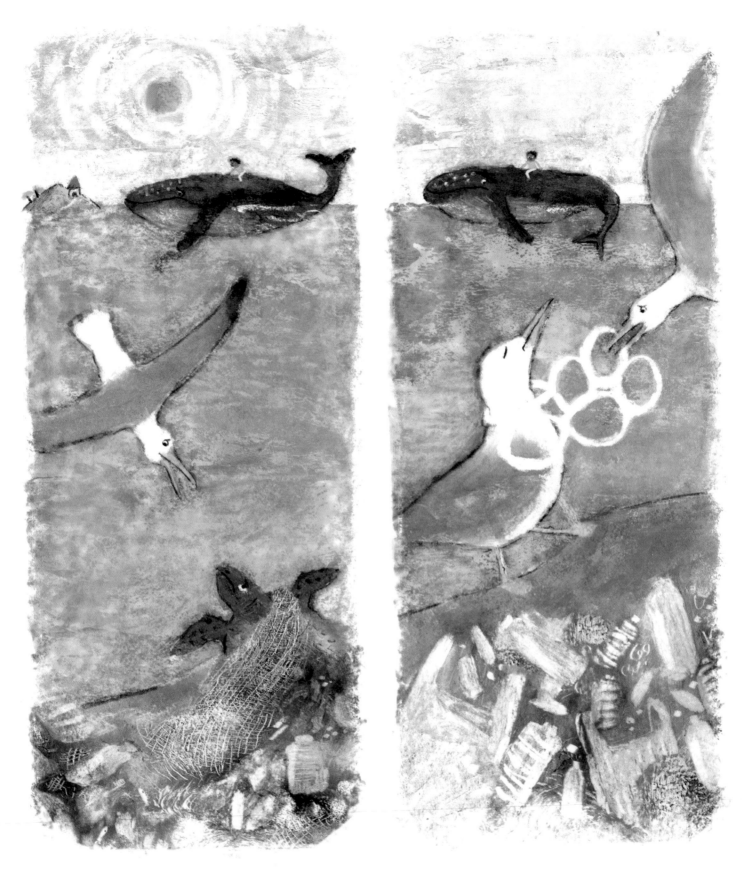

A turtle in trouble,   a gull in distress,

A tightening collar,   a shopping bag mess.

We travelled home saddened
by all we could see . . .
I cried with the whale
and the whale cried with me.

I gazed in his eyes as I stood on the sand,
And made him a promise to tell the whole land

The tale of the whale and the plastic soup sea —

You've heard the whale's story . . .

Please, change it with me.

For Pickle Lilly and Scallywag Magoo – K.S

For Susan and Russell Meek – P

First published in Great Britain in 2021 by Scallywag Press Ltd,
10 Sutherland Row, London SW1V 4JT

This paperback edition published in 2022

Text copyright © 2021 by Karen Swann
Illustration © 2021 by Padmacandra

The rights of Karen Swann and Padmacandra to be identified
as the author and illustrator of this work have been asserted by them
in accordance with the Copyright, Designs and Patents Act, 1988

Printed on FSC paper by OZgraf, Poland

001

British Library Cataloguing in Publication Data available
ISBN 978-1912650-91-0

The Tale
the
Whale

A book to share from
Scallywag Press